Samuel French Acting Edition

The Substance of Bliss

by Tony Glazer

I0591824

‖ SAMUEL FRENCH ‖

SAMUELFRENCH.COM   SAMUELFRENCH.CO.UK

FOR PRODUCTION ENQUIRIES

UNITED STATES AND CANADA
Info@SamuelFrench.com
1-866-598-8449

UNITED KINGDOM AND EUROPE
Plays@SamuelFrench.co.uk
020-7255-4302

Each title is subject to availability from Samuel French, depending upon country of performance. Please be aware that *THE SUBSTANCE OF BLISS* may not be licensed by Samuel French in your territory. Professional and amateur producers should contact the nearest Samuel French office or licensing partner to verify availability.

MUSIC USE NOTE

Licensees are solely responsible for obtaining formal written permission from copyright owners to use copyrighted music in the performance of this play and are strongly cautioned to do so. If no such permission is obtained by the licensee, then the licensee must use only original music that the licensee owns and controls. Licensees are solely responsible and liable for all music clearances and shall indemnify the copyright owners of the play(s) and their licensing agent, Samuel French, against any costs, expenses, losses and liabilities arising from the use of music by licensees. Please contact the appropriate music licensing authority in your territory for the rights to any incidental music.

IMPORTANT BILLING AND CREDIT REQUIREMENTS

If you have obtained performance rights to this title, please refer to your licensing agreement for important billing and credit requirements.

THE SUBSTANCE OF BLISS premiered at the New Jersey Repertory Company in Long Branch, New Jersey on January 14, 2016 under the direction of Evan Bergman. Set design by Jessica Parks. Lighting design by Jill Nagle. Sound design by Merek Royce Press. Costume design by Patricia E. Doherty. Technical Director, Brian Snyder. Stage Manager, Jennifer Tardibuono. The cast was as follows:

DONNA . . . . Susan Maris

PAUL . . . . Christopher Daftsios

CHARACTERS

DONNA (thirties) – Sweet and a little neurotic. Bad temper. Married to Paul.

PAUL (thirties) – Good-natured. Sardonic wit. Married to Donna.

SETTING

The action takes place in the backyard of Donna and Paul's home somewhere in suburban America. It is late at night.

TIME

The present

*(Lights up on a backyard somewhere in suburban America. Lawn furniture, potted plants, and some gardening equipment litter the yard. A man, **PAUL**, walks out into the yard. He carries a rag in his hand. He looks up at the sky – it's late at night, closer to morning. He sits down in one of the lawn chairs.)*

*(A woman, **DONNA**, walks out. Both **DONNA** and **PAUL** have an exhausted but anxiety-wrought energy to them.)*

DONNA. That takes care of the windows.

*(She carries two glasses of water. She hands **PAUL** a glass and sits down in the lawn chair next to him.)*

PAUL. How long do you think it's been since we cleaned them last?

*(**DONNA** stops and considers this.)*

(Finally:)

DONNA. Since we bought them.

PAUL. We cleaned them when we bought them?

DONNA. No, I just meant they were clean when we bought them.

PAUL. Right.

DONNA. Technically, we've never cleaned them.

PAUL. Got it.

(Sipping his water.)

Long time not to clean a thing.

*(**DONNA** does not respond, getting a little tense. She sips her water.)*

How do you neglect something so basic for that long?

7

DONNA. Are you suggesting I don't clean enough?

PAUL. No, not at all… I was just…

DONNA. Because, in this house, it takes three to clean. Not one.

PAUL. I wasn't saying…

DONNA. I'm not the maid, Paul.

PAUL. Don't get your issues all bunched, Donna. I was just wondering how you – not "you" specifically; "you" in general – can see something every day and not think to clean it. How does "one" go along and let something like that happen.

DONNA. I don't know.

PAUL. I don't know, either. That's why I asked. Geez.

DONNA. Okay. Sorry.

PAUL. Thank you.

(**PAUL** *sips his water. A quiet settles, until:*)

DONNA. (*Grudgingly.*) We did let them get pretty filthy, didn't we?

PAUL. (*Looking at his fingers.*) There was this dirt caked onto some of the corners that didn't seem like dirt at all. You could tell that it had been dirt at one time but…it had been there so long that it seemed to have evolved into completely different…stuff. Dirt-*like*. Not primarily dirt anymore, though. It was weird.

(**DONNA** *looks over at* **PAUL.***)

DONNA. It's late. You must be exhausted.

PAUL. Yeah, well…

(*The two look out at the yard in front of them.* **PAUL** *sips his water. He places his glass of water on the ground next to him.* **DONNA** *places her glass of water down next to her.*)

(*A quiet settles, making the two of them anxious, until:*)

DONNA. So…okay…where are we on our list?

PAUL. *(Rubbing his head.)* Well, we've done all the laundry.

DONNA. All the clothes, comforters, curtains.

PAUL. Gave the rugs a beating.

DONNA. Cleaned out the garage. Jess' room.

PAUL. That was a job.

DONNA. Organized all of our receipts for taxes.

PAUL. *(Nodding.)* Business and personal.

DONNA. Did the windows.

PAUL. Check.

DONNA. *(Thinking.)* Is that everything?

PAUL. That's a lot.

DONNA. Wasn't there something else? Where are we on the "home front"?

PAUL. *(Thinking.)* You did want to paint.

DONNA. *(Remembering.)* The living room. I want to paint the living room, that's right. What was the name of the color I liked when we were at the store?

PAUL. "Genteel Pearl."

DONNA. I liked that one.

PAUL. You did.

DONNA. You liked it, too, right?

PAUL. I did.

DONNA. Good color, yes?

PAUL. Sure, it's a good color. Name's a little...

DONNA. *(Overlapping.)* Yeah, but that's what they...

PAUL. *(Overlapping.)* ...Wonky...

DONNA. *(Overlapping.)* ...Do now. They have to do that...

PAUL. *(Overlapping.)* I know, I know. It's *progressive.* That's what they...do...

DONNA. *(Overlapping.)* They have to give it a special name to jazz it up. No one buys "white" anymore.

PAUL. They don't, no. I'm sure.

DONNA. "Genteel Pearl," *yes.* "White"...*not so much.*

PAUL. No, not so much. You're right. Although, technically, white isn't a color. It's more the "absence of color."

DONNA. I think even the "absence of color" can still, technically, be classified as a color. "Genteel Pearl" is a hairsbreadth closer to ivory than traditional white, anyway so...you know...

PAUL. Hm.

> *(Another moment of quiet begins to settle and again, anxiety begins to well up, until:)*

DONNA. So...the living room.

PAUL. Paint the living room.

DONNA. We can go to the store when they open and buy the paint.

PAUL. You think we're still going to be up when the stores open?

DONNA. Well, no, I mean... I meant...*depending...*

PAUL. Okay.

> *(Another quiet, almost painful moment, until:)*

DONNA. With the living room off the list...that would do it, right? That would be everything?

PAUL. I think. Oh...unless you want to do the tin ceiling in the bathroom and in the –

DONNA. *(Overlapping.)* No, I don't think...

PAUL. *(Overlapping.)* ...Hallway.

DONNA. *(Overlapping.)* ...Not now.

PAUL. No?

DONNA. *(Not sure now.)* Well...

PAUL. If we do, we're just going to have to make sure we get the right tiles.

DONNA. The snap ones are good.

PAUL. *(Firm.)* Absolutely not.

DONNA. Paul.

PAUL. No. We cannot use those.

DONNA. They're fine.

PAUL. They're not traditional nail-ups.

DONNA. So?

PAUL. So, if we're going to the trouble to work on this, let's do it the right way. I mean, these are tin ceiling tiles, Donna.

DONNA. You just want an excuse to use the pneumatic gun.

PAUL. What?

DONNA. You're still trying to justify that purchase. This isn't about the "right way." Men and their nail guns. It never ends.

PAUL. That's insulting. I'm insulted. The pneumatic gun is not a toy. It's a very serious tool. And the model I bought is cutting edge.

DONNA. Okay.

PAUL. The ergonomic design alone is worth the price.

DONNA. *Okay.*

PAUL. I'm making a decision based on aesthetic quality. Not a particular tool you just happen to be afraid of.

DONNA. *(Insulted.)* Okay, *fine.*

PAUL. You don't just snap together that kind of look with some drywall screws.

DONNA. *Metal* screws. You don't use drywall screws on a plaster ceiling. You have to use metal screws.

PAUL. *(Defensive.)* I know that. You're purposely…don't act like I don't… I know. My point – that you're allergic to, all of a sudden – is that the tin ceiling tiles you want, in my opinion, are not as nice…you know, we've gone to the trouble of crafting everything else in this house. Let's not cop out now.

DONNA. *Fine.*

PAUL. Plus we have all this other preexisting molding in there. Let's not forget about that. So unless we're taking all that down –

DONNA. No, that molding was there when the house was first built. We agreed we would keep as much of the "old" as possible.

PAUL. Well, okay then, but we are now discussing an "aesthetic mix." We're taking a "new" element and mixing it in with the "old" one. You don't haphazardly throw things together thinking no one will notice. Like with the "different bottles of vodka" fiasco.

DONNA. One time. I did that one time, Paul. I was trying to save space. We had four quarter-filled bottles. I didn't think anyone would notice.

PAUL. I'm just saying that, because of the delicate nature of "aesthetic mixing" –

DONNA. You're making that phrase up.

PAUL. – This requires even more thoughtfulness than just tin ceiling tiles you snap together.

DONNA. We'll be using more filler. You know that, right?

PAUL. Yes, I do. Do you?

DONNA. Yes.

PAUL. *(Suspicious.)* Really?

DONNA. Of course. I know how it works, Paul. We install the tiles from the center to the wall –

PAUL. *(Overlapping.)* I'll install it since you're afraid of the pneumatic gun.

DONNA. – Stopping about six inches shy of the molding and bridging the gap with filler. I get it. I was paying attention at the DIY counter.

PAUL. Fair enough.

> *(Beat.)*

What kind of color tiles are we thinking?

DONNA. How about gold?

PAUL. Gold is "pimpy."

DONNA. Not if we used a "mocha gold."

PAUL. All gold is "pimpy."

DONNA. Since when?

PAUL. Since always. Since the "oldest profession in the world" sought out management.

DONNA. Is that how it went down? Interesting spin you've got there.

PAUL. I don't like gold.

DONNA. We'll look at the colors when we go to the store to buy the paint. We can decide then.

PAUL. Good.

(*Beat.* **DONNA** *considers something.*)

DONNA. You don't think we're in danger of doing too much, do you?

PAUL. How so?

DONNA. Well, theoretically speaking, you get to a point when you renovate past the value of your own home.

PAUL. Oh, I don't think we've done that.

DONNA. No, no, neither do I. Not yet. Just something to watch, is all, I guess.

PAUL. Sure.

(*Beat. The two sit there for a moment, quiet, until:*)

DONNA. That's it, then? On our list?

PAUL. I think so.

DONNA. For now, anyway.

PAUL. Of course.

DONNA. We accomplished quite a bit today and tonight.

PAUL. We have.

(*Pause.*)

(*The two of them go back to their glasses of water, sipping at them.*)

(*The anxiety resumes, this time building, until:*)

DONNA. You're sure he'll come in this way? I mean, assuming he comes home at all, are you sure he'll come in through the back?

PAUL. He did last time.

DONNA. Okay.

PAUL. I think it's his preferred method of entrance.

DONNA. What if he comes in through the front door? Or a side window? To his bedroom? You know, once he gets in his bedroom and locks his door it becomes a whole other... *issue.*

PAUL. I know.

DONNA. And if he has that hammer with him it becomes... you know how he likes to... I mean...

PAUL. We could've taken the locks off the door. We still can.

DONNA. No, we went to the trouble of ordering those antique crystal doorknob lock sets online. We replaced every doorknob in the house and now everything looks clean and uniform. Very timeless and understated. We remove his lock set from the door...the whole look comes apart...it just becomes trashy. The thought makes me squirm. No. We just have to be sure.

PAUL. Do you want me to wait out front? You stay back here?

DONNA. No. You're probably right.

PAUL. Okay. Did you call the...

DONNA. I did.

PAUL. Good.

DONNA. She's expecting us any time.

PAUL. And if we need "additional help"?

DONNA. They're on standby, too.

> (PAUL *nods.*)

PAUL. We have his things together?

DONNA. I packed his suitcase.

PAUL. Okay.

DONNA. We're set. As soon as he comes home.

PAUL. As...soon...as...

> (*They sip their water. It grows quiet again. This time, there seems to be something painful about it – this quiet.* DONNA *looks around the yard, the anxiety building, until:*)

DONNA. I like it back here.

PAUL. It's nice.

DONNA. We forget how nice it is back here.

PAUL. Well, I wouldn't say...not so much forget.

DONNA. Remember.

PAUL. That's...closer.

DONNA. Yeah, I always catch glimpses of it from the kitchen window and I don't think much of it when I do...but when I actually come out here and remember...take it in...really take it in...you know?

PAUL. I do.

DONNA. We're not back here enough.

PAUL. No.

DONNA. We really should try to take more time.

> (PAUL *nods and sips his water. Again more quiet, until:*)

Do you like it? The yard?

PAUL. Yeah.

DONNA. I mean, what we've done with it? Do you like what we've done with it?

PAUL. Absolutely, yes.

DONNA. Okay.

PAUL. I like it.

DONNA. I just worry that I pushed you into all of it – with the landscaping and all the contractors and workers.

PAUL. Not all of them were alcoholics as I remember.

DONNA. No, no...

PAUL. It's fine, really.

DONNA. I just don't want to think that I got you into all of this against your will or that I was being too –

PAUL. No, no you weren't...at all.

> (*Beat.*)

DONNA. So you're happy with everything we've done back here?

PAUL. Very.

DONNA. Okay, good.

> *(Beat.)*

PAUL. Yeah, you know…love the pondless waterfall.

DONNA. Me too.

PAUL. The gazebo-style bird feeder.

DONNA. All the perennials in our garden.

PAUL. Bamboo plant with the root guard.

> (**DONNA** *looks around the yard, proud.*)

DONNA. We've really made it our own.

PAUL. We have.

DONNA. I like it.

PAUL. The yard looks great.

DONNA. It does look great, huh?

PAUL. You were right to want to reimagine it again back here.

DONNA. *(Proud.)* I was.

PAUL. *(Sincere.)* Take a bow.

> *(Again more quiet. The anxiety building once again, until:)*

DONNA. Even the fairy?

PAUL. Even the fairy.

DONNA. I know how you feel about fairies.

PAUL. For the record, I don't think I really feel any particular way about them.

DONNA. They're not your favorite.

PAUL. True. No. I'm not a fan of fairies. No one could accuse me of that.

DONNA. Looks good, though, right? The fairy?

PAUL. Sure, I mean, as far as "fairies" go…I think this was a definite…way to go…with the fairy and the wings and…all the other "fairy paraphernalia"…

> *(Pointing.)*

...I don't exactly know what that part is...specifically...

DONNA. It's a wand.

PAUL. Oh, I thought maybe it was a stick.

DONNA. No, wand. Magic wand.

PAUL. Of course. That makes sense.

DONNA. To bless the house. I just wanted to bless the house.

PAUL. With a fairy, sure. I get that now.

DONNA. You like the fairy, right?

PAUL. *(Overlapping.)* Well, I don't...

DONNA. *(Overlapping.)* You don't like it.

PAUL. *(Overlapping.)* ...It's not that...I mean, that's *your*...

DONNA. We can get rid of her.

PAUL. No, no, I'm not saying that...at all.

DONNA. Is she too *new-agey*? Is that it?

PAUL. It does get a little bit...in that direction...

DONNA. If you're uncomfortable...

PAUL. I'm not uncomfortable. Don't get me...that's not...

DONNA. I want you to be comfortable.

PAUL. I am. I'm comfortable. I'm very comfortable with the fairy. It's a really good...fairy.

DONNA. Good.

(*Beat.*)

PAUL. It was just, you know...you're reading into my initial feeling about it when we first...it was a security thing in the beginning...the weight of it. It's solid stone.

DONNA. It is heavy.

PAUL. Exactly. I just didn't want it to fall over and kill any woodland creatures, you know?

DONNA. I understand.

PAUL. As far as "blessings" go, I didn't think that would be a good omen...you know, crushing a squirrel.

DONNA. We didn't crush a...come on, we fixed it.

PAUL. Yeah, no, the fishing line secures it really well. You don't even see it, really, and I think it's safe…now. So… I'm fine with it.

DONNA. I like her. I really like her.

PAUL. Yeah.

DONNA. Should we name her?

PAUL. *(Firm.)* No.

DONNA. You don't think she should have a name?

PAUL. I think…as far as "magical beings" go they already have an "otherworldly" name…so…

DONNA. Just let her…have that?

PAUL. Yeah, we don't need to name it.

DONNA. Her.

PAUL. I think she's fine.

DONNA. Okay.

> *(Pause. Suddenly,* DONNA *cocks her head.)*

PAUL. What's wrong?

DONNA. Did you hear that?

PAUL. What? No…did you…?

DONNA. *(Putting her hand up.)* Shh.

> *(The two sit there for a moment, listening.)*

PAUL. I'm not…

DONNA. Shh.

> *(Again more listening, until:)*

I definitely think I heard something out front.

> *(*PAUL *stands up and moves toward the front of the house.)*

PAUL. Okay. Hang tight.

DONNA. *(Standing up.)* Should I…

PAUL. No, no. Stay here. Just in case.

DONNA. Okay. Hurry.

> *(*PAUL *exits, heading toward the front of the house. It's quiet.)*

Paul?

>*(More quiet settles.)*

Come on, come on, come on...

>*(**DONNA** is a jangle of nerves, until:)*
>
>*(**PAUL** comes back, shaking his head.)*

No?

PAUL. I didn't see anything.

DONNA. I thought I heard him.

PAUL. *(Agitated.)* Nothing.

>*(The both sit back down in their chairs.)*

DONNA. What's wrong?

PAUL. *(Distracted.)* What?

DONNA. You look agitated.

PAUL. Oh. No, it's just Aaron and his damn "Elect Jameson" sign in his front yard. Every time I see it, it's like a multicolored finger thump to my eyeball.

DONNA. The colors from that sign really clash with the balusters on his porch.

PAUL. *(Getting worked up.)* And he has to leave his porch light on all night so any random passersby can know his politics...it's just so amazingly...obnoxious.

DONNA. Well, free country has its price.

PAUL. Libertarians.

DONNA. Don't get yourself toxic, Paul.

PAUL. It's the principle of it.

DONNA. The principle of it will spike your IBS.

>*(**PAUL** huffs a small, weary laugh. He grabs his glass.)*

PAUL. You're right.

DONNA. Imagine that.

PAUL. Smart-ass.

DONNA. Thank you, dear.

(PAUL *sips at his water. A quiet begins to settle, until:*)

DONNA. I really thought I heard something.

(PAUL *shakes his head, placing his glass back down.*)

(*More quiet, until:*)

Are you sure you didn't see anything out front?

PAUL. I'm sure.

DONNA. I could've sworn...

(*Again, a quiet settles.*)

PAUL. I did smell that skunk.

DONNA. I can't believe that thing is still wandering around here.

PAUL. Probably thinks the same thing about us.

DONNA. That smell...

PAUL. Probably thinks the same thing about us.

DONNA. And it's the only one, right?

PAUL. As far as we know, it's just the one.

DONNA. It's been years. How long do skunks live, anyway?

PAUL. No idea.

DONNA. Such a pain.

PAUL. We could call Animal Control again.

DONNA. No. They never find it and then they just get all...

PAUL. Yeah.

DONNA. ..."In our face" about it. Like it's our fault they can't find it.

PAUL. You spend your days dealing with rabid raccoons and pit bulls, I think it starts to rub off on you.

DONNA. Yeah, but...

PAUL. Occupational hazard, that kind of hostility.

DONNA. Just doesn't seem fair.

PAUL. Your tax dollars at work.

(*Quiet settles again, this one a little more intense, until:*)

DONNA. Do you think he's hurt? As we're talking, do you think he's physically in danger? He's small for his age... plus all his allergies...and now this...do you think he's in trouble?

(PAUL *doesn't respond. A painful quiet settles, until:*)

I walked into his room earlier today. Just checking to see if anything else needed to be done in there...and even though we scrubbed the whole area down from top to bottom...it just didn't seem clean, you know?

PAUL. Yeah.

DONNA. All that scrubbing and bleaching...there still seems to be some kind of a...*film*...all over everything. I know that sounds crazy...it just seemed there was a part of the room we just couldn't get at...break down... clean up...you see that, too? There's something there, right? Is it me? Am I just...projecting?

PAUL. No, I don't think you're...it's strange in there...it's not you...there's a real...something...in there...

DONNA. Okay.

PAUL. Definitely not you.

(*More quiet.* DONNA *begins to become visibly upset. She takes a breath.*)

DONNA. We should build a pool back here.

PAUL. A pool?

DONNA. A pool.

PAUL. What about the waterfall?

DONNA. We can't swim in that.

PAUL. No. I just thought we had covered "water" back here already with that.

DONNA. Maybe we could substitute the waterfall with an actual pool. Of water. For us.

PAUL. We don't have that much room back here.

DONNA. It doesn't have to be an Olympic-size pool or anything.

PAUL. I wouldn't want an above ground pool.

DONNA. Dear God, no. Of course not. I wouldn't be caught...

PAUL. Inground pool.

DONNA. Yes. A nice inground pool with polymer walls and a heat pump...maybe get a custom shape out of it... something tasteful...different...that still compliments the space...that's in harmony with it.

PAUL. No fairy shapes.

DONNA. No, not a fairy but something...an angel, maybe...

PAUL. Angels are fairies.

DONNA. That's not technically true.

PAUL. Shape-wise it is.

DONNA. Well, okay then, not an angel but maybe... I don't know...how about...how about...

PAUL. How about oval?

DONNA. Oval is boring.

PAUL. Sorry.

DONNA. It's a very boring shape.

PAUL. Guess. *(Getting an idea.)* Remember when we went on that trip to the DR? That all-inclusive resort we were at and we spent all our time by the pool?

DONNA. I loved that pool.

PAUL. How about a shape like that? That wasn't boring.

DONNA. *(Thinking.)* What would you call a shape like that?

PAUL. Oh...uh..."Resort Shape"...we could draw it for someone to make for us. We could go to one of those custom places and have them make it like that.

DONNA. That was a big pool.

PAUL. We could make a smaller version.

DONNA. I loved that pool.

PAUL. Me too.

DONNA. That was such a great trip.

PAUL. It was.

DONNA. I felt so…

PAUL. Rested.

DONNA. We ate so much food.

PAUL. *(Blissful.)* I know.

DONNA. We'd lie by the pool with our little "food babies" and stacks of books and just luxuriate in it…feeling so…content. It was such a perfect trip.

PAUL. Until your mom called your cell phone.

DONNA. *(Remembering.)* She'll never watch Jess again. She doesn't even visit anymore.

PAUL. None of our parents do.

> *(Quiet settles.* DONNA *begins to become upset again, until:)*

DONNA. So we'll get a pool.

PAUL. We'll look into it.

DONNA. Don't humor me.

PAUL. I'm not.

DONNA. I think it would be good to get a pool. Humoring is not appropriate.

PAUL. I wouldn't do that. We'll call someone tomorrow.

DONNA. Okay. Good. Good.

> *(Again, more quiet.)*

We've checked everywhere, right? Emergency rooms, jails…

PAUL. All the greatest hits.

DONNA. We haven't missed a spot, have we?

PAUL. Not that I can think of. Drove by all his hangout spots.

DONNA. Right, right.

PAUL. Friends' houses. Girlfriends. We've looked everywhere.

DONNA. Okay, okay.

> *(More quiet.* DONNA *once more seems to be fighting something. She takes a breath.)*

DONNA. Did we do something wrong?

PAUL. No.

DONNA. Is he punishing us for something we did?

PAUL. Of course not...look, you know this...*we know this already*. The first thing parents want to do is blame themselves.

DONNA. I know.

PAUL. All those meetings we went to in the beginning... *everyone*...every meeting was like watching the same response on a loop...it's the first thing they...and we talked about this, Donna.

DONNA. But what if we're wrong?

PAUL. We're not.

DONNA. We've been wrong about everything else with him. Why would we think we're right now?

PAUL. I don't think we're wrong about this.

DONNA. Are we handling it wrong now?

PAUL. How does one handle something like this? No one gives you a...look, we're trying, okay? We're doing the best we can.

DONNA. It doesn't feel like we're doing enough.

PAUL. Because nothing we're doing is working but that doesn't mean...it doesn't mean we're wrong.

DONNA. So we stop trying?

PAUL. No, but...we can stop covering old ground.

(*Another moment of quiet begins to settle, until:*)

DONNA. Why would he do this to himself? He has so much going for him. I mean, fashion-wise, he doesn't have a clue...

PAUL. He doesn't.

DONNA. We've had to keep his sense of clothing style in check periodically...he is an "autumn."

PAUL. Right.

DONNA. And that whole thing about wanting to be a marine biologist was just...silly. We had to intervene there.

PAUL. Of course.

DONNA. But other than that he's a great kid.

PAUL. He is.

DONNA. I can't understand it. He's so smart and funny and kind and...and...and he wants to throw it away. All that...he wants to throw it away like it doesn't mean anything...like he's some...piece of meat...a piece of garbage.

PAUL. I don't think there's a rational explanation to any of this.

DONNA. The hell with him, then.

PAUL. Donna.

DONNA. Seriously, Paul. We give him everything he wants and this is how he repays us?

PAUL. Come on.

DONNA. No, I'm sorry. We raised him to be more reasonable than that.

PAUL. It's an unreasonable drug.

DONNA. Screw him and that drug.

PAUL. Don't say that.

DONNA. *(Suddenly panicked.)* Do you think he's prostituting himself? For drugs? Do you think he's selling himself in a bus station bathroom?

PAUL. No.

DONNA. How can you be so sure?

PAUL. His game system is still here. His tablet is still in his room. So is his laptop. Surely he'd sell those things before going down on someone at the bus station.

DONNA. But that's rational. You said yourself there's no way to rationally address any of this.

PAUL. I didn't exactly mean...

DONNA. He's sucking off a trucker.

PAUL. Donna, my God.

DONNA. No, I know it. Our beautiful baby son is sucking off some fat, greasy trucker in a bathroom. Knee-level in a bathroom stall...the smells he must be experiencing.

PAUL. Just try to –

DONNA. Maybe he's letting them screw him. I read about this. They're called "bottoms." Maybe he's being someone's "bottom" for drug money.

PAUL. Thank you for that lovely image, Donna. That is now permanently burned on my retinas.

(DONNA *looks over at* PAUL, *suspicious.*)

DONNA. How can you be so calm about this?

PAUL. Neither of us can afford to be freaking out right now. He will probably be home any minute and we're going to have to be together when he does.

DONNA. What if he doesn't come home?

(*This last thought hangs there, until:*)

PAUL. Let's just…can we get on the same page? We just need to calm down and be on the same page.

DONNA. Okay.

PAUL. Can we do that?

DONNA. Yes, okay…you're right… I'm just being…

PAUL. You are.

DONNA. *Okay.* Sorry.

PAUL. Thank you.

DONNA. I just get…

PAUL. I know.

DONNA. I get a little…

PAUL. It's understandable.

(*A quiet settles, until:*)

DONNA. It's good you're here.

PAUL. Of course I'm here.

DONNA. It really is.

(*Something catches* PAUL*'s eye.*)

PAUL. (*Distracted.*) Uh-huh.

DONNA. You keep me…grounded, you know? You've always been…

(**PAUL** *stands up.* **DONNA** *does not notice.*)

PAUL. *(To himself.)* Wait…where's the…?

DONNA. I don't know what I would do if you weren't so… cool-headed, so level about things.

(**PAUL** *moves downstage.*)

PAUL. *(Angry.)* Oh, for the love of… Donna.

DONNA. What? What is it? What's wrong?

PAUL. *(Accusing.)* You tell me.

DONNA. What? I don't…

PAUL. Where is it, Donna?

DONNA. *(Guilty.)* Where is what?

PAUL. Don't play that. Don't you play that with me.

DONNA. I'm not playing anything.

PAUL. You know exactly what I'm talking about, Donna. Where is it?

(**DONNA** *takes a moment. Finally:*)

DONNA. Well…

PAUL. What do you mean, "well"?

DONNA. I don't like that thing.

PAUL. Oh, come on.

DONNA. It's evil.

PAUL. What did you do with it?

DONNA. I took it down. I took it apart and I took it down.

PAUL. Where is it?

DONNA. It's in the garage.

PAUL. It was out there to keep… I installed that… I bought and installed that to keep those damn…

DONNA. Don't talk about them like that.

PAUL. …Those goddamn cats out of our yard and you…

DONNA. It's cruel.

PAUL. It's not – for God's sake, Donna – we agreed on this.

DONNA. I like the cats.

PAUL. They are shitting in our yard.

DONNA. Cats do that.

PAUL. They don't have to do that in our yard.

DONNA. You're so cruel about cats, Paul. That's a bad sign, you know.

PAUL. *(Overlapping.)* Disgusting little...shit.

DONNA. *(Overlapping.)* That's "serial killer" bad. Did you have some bad experience with them as a child?

PAUL. I'm having a bad experience with them right now.

DONNA. You're being ridiculous.

PAUL. I just don't want our backyard smelling like a litter box. Is that too much to ask? We've spent a lot of money back here – money we don't necessarily have.

DONNA. I know, but I can't help it. They're cute, Paul. I see them and I just want to hold them.

PAUL. *(Murderous.)* Believe me, I want to hold them, too.

DONNA. Stop. They have very adorable qualities.

PAUL. They have the shitting capacity of a horse.

DONNA. Why are you so concerned about the safety of the squirrels in the area but not the outdoor cats?

PAUL. Don't do that. Do not call them "outdoor cats" just to legitimize their behavior. You don't call hoboes, "outdoor people."

DONNA. Stop changing the subject, Paul.

PAUL. I'm not changing anything.

DONNA. No, no, no. Let's stay on this. You made such a big thing about the possibility of the fairy falling on any "woodland creatures" and yet you could apparently care less about the cats in our neighborhood.

PAUL. Cats are not "woodland creatures." By definition they're not indigenous to the area. They're domesticated "clap traps" let loose to shit their way across the neighborhood.

DONNA. Squirrels poop, too, you know.

PAUL. Have you ever seen a squirrel shit?

DONNA. Well, no...not exactly.

PAUL. Do you know why?

DONNA. I know you're about to say something really obnoxious.

PAUL. Because wherever they shit, they're not shitting here. That skunk doesn't even come back here to do its business. That means we have a natural understanding about things. They shit in their own place and on their own time. They don't make it my problem by shitting in my yard.

DONNA. *Our* yard.

PAUL. Exactly. You have a stake in this, too. Why don't you care about the flow of excrement back here?

DONNA. I swear, Paul. You get so self-righteous about this. I hate how you can get.

PAUL. We spend all this money, Donna. We go into a financial deficit to make everything look nice, only to have...

(**PAUL** *sees something else. He walks downstage.*)

DONNA. What's the matter?

PAUL. Great.

DONNA. Now what?

PAUL. Is that what I think it is?

DONNA . What are you talking about?

(**PAUL** *stops and points.*)

PAUL. What is that?

DONNA. What is what?

PAUL. *(Pointing.) That.* What is that, Donna?

(**DONNA** *walks over to where* **PAUL** *is standing and looks to where he is pointing.*)

DONNA. Oh...

PAUL. Jesus, Donna, really?

DONNA. Paul.

PAUL. This is exactly what I'm talking about.

DONNA. I didn't do anything wrong.

PAUL. Oh no?

DONNA. No.

PAUL. Then what is it?

DONNA. Well...

PAUL. Tell me. Tell me what that is? You haven't done anything wrong? Fine. What is that, then?

DONNA. It...looks like it might be...cat...stuff.

PAUL. Shit. Cat shit. Mustang-size cat shit. These are mustang-size, shitting cats, Donna. And from where exactly do you think this mustang-size cat shit may have come?

DONNA. A cat.

PAUL. Bravo. It came from a cat. Well done.

DONNA. You're such a jerk.

PAUL. You know, you think you're the "cat whisperer" Donna, but when you get right down to it, you are the "cat shit whisperer." That's what you are.

DONNA. That's...that's just nonsense.

PAUL. It's "true-sense" because at the end of the day, when all is said and done, you've turned our entire yard into a toilet for *kittens.*

DONNA. Okay Paul, you've made your point.

(**PAUL** *begins sniffing suspiciously.*)

PAUL. What is that?

DONNA. What is what?

PAUL. Do you smell that?

DONNA. I don't smell...

PAUL. Wait a minute...wait a minute...

DONNA. There's not...you can't smell...

(**PAUL** *walks over to another part of the yard.*)

PAUL. There's cat piss in our yard now. I can smell it.

DONNA. You can't smell that.

PAUL. I'm smelling it right now, Donna!

DONNA. Paul.

PAUL. This is why I bought that machine.

DONNA. I don't like that machine.

PAUL. That machine was keeping all the mutant waste out of our yard.

DONNA. It was *zapping* them.

PAUL. It was not *zapping* them, Donna.

DONNA. It was a *zap*.

PAUL. It was not a *zap*. It was a "firm but safe electrical current" that humanely discouraged them from spending time in our yard.

DONNA. I don't care what the back of the box said, it was hurting them.

PAUL. Well, look who's hurting us now!

DONNA. Why are you so mad about this?

PAUL. Because you've gone on this renovation spree back here – *again* – and never once have I told you no. Now you want to get a pool with a polymer lining and a heat pump and no doubt before we're through here, you're going to want a built-in slide –

DONNA. Diving board's better.

PAUL. And I'm going to say *yes*. I'm going to say yes because I say yes to everything back here but the one thing that I wanted, the one thing that I made a personal request for and you have to go and veto that without even telling me.

DONNA. Paul.

PAUL. No, we've spent a lot of money to get our yard looking nice and even more money to keep those damn things out and now you've taken away the one thing – *my only request* – you've just unilaterally dismissed my input on this and now they're running wild back here again!

DONNA. I like cats.

PAUL. So we'll buy a cat.

DONNA. I don't want a cat in the house, Paul. You end up having fur everywhere, you have to have a litter box and it smells.

PAUL. But the shit smell's okay out here? Unbelievable.

DONNA. I don't understand something, Paul. You have this cool, calm, rational head when it comes to Jess...

PAUL. Where the...whoa, wait a minute...

DONNA. *(Overlapping.)* But when it comes to random neighborhood cats, you're an emotional typhoon.

PAUL. *(Overlapping.)* I already told you about that...this isn't...

DONNA. You fly into a rage about the cat stuff in our yard but not our son's stuff in our life.

PAUL. This isn't the same thing...you can't compare the two...

DONNA. You're freaking out about neighborhood cats but when are you going to lose your temper like that for our son?

PAUL. This is apples and oranges, Donna. You're turning this on its head.

DONNA. At least I'm doing something! I'm not sitting around like some sad, retarded Zen Cow.

PAUL. "Sad, retarded Zen Cow"? Really, Donna? I'm meant to defend myself against a statement like that?

DONNA. Aren't you upset about this, Paul?

PAUL. Of course I'm upset.

DONNA. Doesn't our son being in harm's way do something to you?

PAUL. What kind of question is that?

DONNA. Aren't you angry that he's done this to himself?

PAUL. What good is being angry about this?

DONNA. What good is being angry about the neighborhood cats?

PAUL. *(Overlapping.)* It's not the same thing. Stop doing that...

DONNA. *(Overlapping.)* He's our son! Jess is...

PAUL. *(Overlapping.)* I know who our son is, goddammit.

DONNA. *(Overlapping.)* Out there somewhere, God-only-knows where, all whacked out on that drug – that *fucking drug* – and you're carrying on about the neighborhood cats!

PAUL. Our *son's* shit is very involved. The *cat* shit had a resolution, it was off our list and you purposely screwed it all up.

DONNA. So what are you saying? Our son's problem is too complex to get upset about?

PAUL. Don't do that. I hate when you... I'm not saying that. You're saying that – *and you know it.* The truth is, I caught you in a deception and instead of addressing it, all you want to do is change the subject!

DONNA. I'm not changing the subject! Our son is the subject! It's the only reason we're up at this hour! It's the only reason we're cleaning and organizing and reorganizing! Our son! It's the only reason you're in the yard right now to even know I dismantled your little "Mengele Machine." Our son is the subject, Paul!

(A light turns on from a neighbor's house next door.)

PAUL. We woke up Mrs. Johnston.

DONNA. You woke her up.

PAUL. Turn out the lights.

DONNA. *(Heading toward the light switch.)* Don't you tell me what to do.

PAUL. Come on, hurry up.

(DONNA turns out the backyard light and the two sit back down in their chairs. After a moment, we hear the sounds of a back door opening.)

(DONNA and PAUL push themselves down a little farther in their chairs. They speak in hushed tones.)

PAUL. She will make such a stink at the next planning committee.

DONNA. Not if you stop talking.

PAUL. Shh.

DONNA. *You* shh. Don't you shh me.

PAUL. *Shh.*

> *(Finally, the sound of a door closing is heard. A few moments after that, the light goes out. They relax and resume speaking in normal tones.)*

We would have never heard the end of that. She would have beelined right over to us at the next planning committee and it would have been, "Yes, Mrs. Johnston. No, Mrs. Johnston. We're very sorry, Mrs. Johnston."

DONNA. Why do we call her Mrs. Johnston, anyway? Why don't we just call her Claire? That is her first name.

PAUL. She prefers "Mrs. Johnston."

DONNA. Yeah, but we're all adults.

PAUL. I don't think she views it that way.

DONNA. Apparently not.

PAUL. We're not from that generation.

DONNA. Which generation is that?

PAUL. Umm…the one…we're not a part of?

DONNA. That's just…dumb.

PAUL. You know, she's so unpleasant, I'm happy it's that cordial. She's actually doing us a favor.

DONNA. She never takes care of that yard of hers.

PAUL. She is "yard challenged."

DONNA. The rose bushes and that grass…she just lets it all grow wild. And it's not just the rose bushes and grass… she's got a real science project growing over there. I peeked over there the other day and I couldn't tell what half of it was.

PAUL. Well, that's why we got the higher fence. So we don't have to see it.

DONNA. Still…

> *(Quiet.)*

So. Where were we?

PAUL. Waiting. We're waiting.

(Another quiet begins to settle, until:)

DONNA. I meant with our fight. Before we woke up Mrs. Johnston.

PAUL. I'm putting that machine back together.

DONNA. Can't you find a "non-zapping" one? Please, Paul. That really bothers me.

(PAUL considers this.)

(Finally:)

PAUL. I'll look online.

DONNA. Thank you.

(Again, a quiet begins to settle. Then:)

That wasn't the part I was talking about, actually. I was talking about the other part of our fight.

PAUL. Oh.

DONNA. Yes. So?

PAUL. We just don't process these things the same way, Donna. You're more...on your sleeve with everything... I just want to keep things in a certain place so I can maintain perspective. If I can have it in front of me, outside of me, not so close to me...I can work through it a little better.

DONNA. How's that working for you?

PAUL. How's melting down working for you?

(They give each other a look that says "truce" before looking out at the backyard in front of them.)

(Once again, quiet begins to consume them, until:)

DONNA. Do you think Mrs. Johnston suspects we're the ones who woke her up? I mean, she walked right up to the edge of our fence...like she thought it was us. It seemed like she had something, too...like a step ladder or something because I could just make out the top of her head trying to peek over and see.

(**PAUL** *doesn't respond.*)

DONNA. Do you think she suspects us?

PAUL. Let's not look a gift horse in the anus.

DONNA. Charming.

PAUL. I'm just saying, without proof that we woke her up, we're safe at the next planning committee.

DONNA. When is the next planning committee?

PAUL. Tuesday.

DONNA. Already? Seems like we just had one.

PAUL. Nope. Tuesday.

(*Some more quiet, until:*)

DONNA. I know being on this committee was a good idea in theory...

PAUL. Yeah...

DONNA. ...But I have to tell you, now that we're part of the actual planning of things in this town, I find myself questioning everything.

PAUL. Me too. I didn't care about half the things this town did until I was suddenly on a committee for it.

DONNA. Like this year's fair. Every year we've gone to this fair – every year since we've moved here – and it hasn't been until we got on the planning committee for it that I realized certain things about it.

(*She thinks about this.*)

Do you even know who Saint Rocco is?

PAUL. He's the Patron Saint of Pestilence.

DONNA. You knew that?

PAUL. I looked online.

DONNA. Yeah, but did you look online before or after you were on the committee for it?

PAUL. After.

DONNA. See that? That's what I'm talking about.

PAUL. I know.

DONNA. What the hell is that?

PAUL. That I don't know.

DONNA. It's like before we were on the committee we would go, every year, to the "Saint Rocco's *Fair*" but now that we're on the committee, we're going to the... "Saint *Rocco's* Fair," and suddenly I'm like, "Who the hell is Saint *Rocco?*"

PAUL. Pestilence.

DONNA. Huh.

PAUL. Although there was another website that said he was the Patron Saint of Dogs so I'm not exactly sure. It's one of those two. Pestilence or Dogs.

DONNA. That's a big difference.

PAUL. Depends where the pestilence came from.

DONNA. I think it's the name that bugs me. Rocco. Saint Rocco. It's weird.

PAUL. I guess.

DONNA. Don't you think it's a little "*Godfather* meets Jesus"?

PAUL. *(Weary.)* I don't know, Donna. They're Catholics. They have a saint for everything.

DONNA. They don't have one for our son.

PAUL. They do, actually.

DONNA. Really?

PAUL. After I looked up Rocco, I just sort of went on a "search engine jag." Saint Maximilian Kolbe. Patron Saint of Drug Addicts and Families.

DONNA. Does that translate to "Families of Drug Addicts"?

PAUL. If it doesn't, I think, at the very least, it puts it in the same department.

DONNA. Too bad we're not Catholic.

PAUL. "In the name of the Father...the Son..."

DONNA. *(Indicating Mrs. Johnston.)* She still thinks we are, though, right? For all she knows we're Catholic, yeah?

PAUL. I don't think she suspects anything different.

DONNA. Good. Yeah.

> *(Quiet settles in, until:)*

DONNA. Those Catholics.

PAUL. I know.

DONNA. They have it all worked out, don't they?

PAUL. Two thousand years don't lie.

DONNA. Two thousand and counting. Amazing run.

PAUL. It really is.

DONNA. It's because they're so organized. Very organized. Very detailed. Right down to a saint for drug addicts. Very impressive. The detail of it. We could really learn something from them.

>   *(Quiet ensues, until:)*

I wonder if that would help. Praying to a saint for drug addicts.

PAUL. *(Joking.)* We could always cross over and give it a shot. We're running out of ideas on our own, anyway.

>   **(DONNA** *looks over at* **PAUL,** *annoyed.)*

DONNA. Is that supposed to be funny?

PAUL. Only incidentally.

DONNA. Meaning?

PAUL. Meaning it's true. It just also happens to be funny but the intent was to state a truth not a joke.

DONNA. So what's the joke part? "Friendly fire"?

PAUL. I would prefer, "unintended consequence."

DONNA. Of course you would.

PAUL. Are we fighting again?

>   *(It's quiet again. As the quiet builds, it becomes almost unbearable for them to just sit. The waiting is taking its toll.)*
>
>   *(Finally:)*

DONNA. It's his birthday next week.

PAUL. I know.

DONNA. I thought about getting him something. Don't you think we should get him something?

PAUL. He is getting "all-inclusive rehab." That is "something." Sure cost "something."

DONNA. I meant like a real present.

PAUL. Ah. One of those.

DONNA. I was at the mall over by "Zingers and Things" the other day and I was walking around looking for a store that might have something he'd like and I realized I have no idea what our son likes, what he would want as a present. Do you?

PAUL. Certain substances excluded?

DONNA. Obviously.

PAUL. No, actually. I don't.

DONNA. I thought it was just me. Neither of us know. That's wrong, isn't it? Isn't that wrong?

PAUL. On a scale I think it ranks towards the bottom.

DONNA. We should know more about what he likes, Paul. Maybe if we knew more about what he liked –

PAUL. *(Interrupting.)* He wouldn't be doing –

DONNA. *(Interrupting.)* No. I didn't mean that.

PAUL. Because that sounds like a backdoor way of blaming ourselves and I thought we were past that.

DONNA. I'm not. We are.

PAUL. So what's your point?

DONNA. Did we ever know what he liked?

PAUL. He's a fifteen-year-old kid. He likes "fifteen-year-old kid" things…and then, when he gets to that "age," he doesn't like anything his parents give him so…

DONNA. Did we ever give him a present he liked?

PAUL. Of course we have. I think. We must have.

DONNA. You know, I talk – correction, rant – about how I can't believe he's doing all these things. But disbelief has to be based on information I have on him already. But did we have any information? I mean, we don't know what kind of gifts he likes. What else don't we know about him?

PAUL. What are you saying? We don't know our own son?

DONNA. No, I...

PAUL. *(Serious.)* Maybe we don't know him.

DONNA. No, no.

PAUL. Seriously, what you just said...that kind of...

DONNA. No, I'm just saying, maybe if we knew more about what he likes, we'd have an easier time talking to him. Maybe we could start talking *with* him and not *at* him. That's all I mean.

PAUL. Maybe.

DONNA. What do boys his age like?

> *(This question hangs there, until:)*

You're a guy.

PAUL. True.

DONNA. What did you like at his age?

PAUL. Girls.

DONNA. Well, we can't get him a hooker, Paul.

PAUL. Who wants to get him a hooker?

DONNA. I'm just saying. He's breaking enough laws as it is.

PAUL. For the record, I wasn't suggesting we get him a hooker.

DONNA. What did you like at his age that could be found at the mall?

> **(PAUL** *thinks about it.)*
>
> *(Finally:)*

PAUL. Girls hang out at the mall.

DONNA. You're no help.

PAUL. Sorry. I remember that age very well. He probably has a lot of interest in girls.

DONNA. Well, then, maybe you should have a conversation with him about it.

PAUL. That'll go over well.

DONNA. Don't get clinical about it. Just find out what kind of girls he's into, what kind of entertainers he thinks are sexy. You know, what kind of porn actresses he streams. You can compare notes on your favorite porn stars when you were growing up. If girls are the common denominator maybe you two can bond on porn.

PAUL. Bond on porn with a minor? Didn't you just chastise me for breaking the law?

DONNA. You know what I mean.

PAUL. I'm not sure what kind of porno stars our son is into but I can almost guarantee they don't have stretch marks.

DONNA. Paul.

PAUL. It's true. With my dad, he could tell me stories about a sex symbol of his day – Marilyn Monroe, for example – and I can look at an old photo of her from back then and totally get it because she left the planet before she got wrinkled. It's not the same with my generation. *Especially with porno stars.* A lot of the porno stars of my youth are still around, they're still in circulation, only they've been re-branded "Cougars," "MILFs." Instead of going gently into that good cum-shot, they've been forced to resurface through some sinister raising of the mandatory retirement age just to make me feel old, irrelevant; unworthy of ever having a hard-on.

DONNA. You're overstating things, I think.

PAUL. My prostate begs to differ.

DONNA. You're not old, Paul.

PAUL. Hey, I'm just as surprised as you but it happened. I don't know when it happened, I don't know how, it just happened... I don't remember when I crossed over. Just that I did. It's like you don't remember the exact moment you stopped believing in Santa Claus or you don't remember when you started actually throwing your popcorn in the trash after the movie instead of just leaving it there on the floor for the usher. You don't remember those changes, those shifts. You just find yourself on the other side of it. Same thing here. One day I'm young, the next day wearing a backpack makes me look creepy.

(Quiet.)

DONNA. Do you remember the moment when we stopped having sex?

PAUL. Where did that come from?

DONNA. Do you?

(Another quiet settles, until:)

PAUL. No.

(Another moment.)

(Finally:)

DONNA. How long has it been?

PAUL. If you have to ask…

DONNA. That's your answer?

PAUL. I don't have an answer.

DONNA. Are you sick of me?

PAUL. Of course not.

(Beat.)

Are you sick of me?

DONNA. No.

PAUL. Okay then.

DONNA. Are you bored?

PAUL. No.

DONNA. What's the problem?

PAUL. We've been dealing with a lot of stress lately.

DONNA. This started before that. Don't blame this on Jess.

PAUL. I'm not blaming anyone. Why does there have to be blame in this?

DONNA. Are you having an affair?

PAUL. With all my free time.

DONNA. Are you?

PAUL. No. Are you?

DONNA. Why would I have an affair?

PAUL. Why would I?

DONNA. Are you fucking your computer?

PAUL. What does that mean?

DONNA. I think you know.

PAUL. No, for God's sake, I am not...*fucking my computer.*

DONNA. Is this just what happens? You're with one person for long enough. Is this the natural evolution of marriage? Is this monogamy's endgame?

PAUL. What does *Cosmo* say?

DONNA. If I wanted misinformation about my sex life, I'd buy an App.

PAUL. Maybe we're just going through a phase or a cycle.

DONNA. Which one is it? A phase? Or a cycle?

PAUL. I don't know.

DONNA. Because a phase we can work out of – it's linear in nature. A cycle means no matter what we do we'll have to go through it all over again.

PAUL. I don't know if it's either of those two. It could be neither of those, you know? It could be one of them or both of them. I don't know what the hell it is.

DONNA. I don't like it.

PAUL. Really? I'm thrilled about it. I get so much more computer time.

DONNA. I didn't sign on for a sexless marriage.

PAUL. I didn't sign on for a drug-addicted son so there you go. I guess we both have buyer's remorse.

> (**DONNA** *takes this in.* **PAUL** *takes this is in, realizing something.*)

DONNA. I don't have...is that what you're...is that what's really going on with you? Is that why you've been so detached – oh, excuse me, level-headed – about everything? Because you're having *buyer's remorse?* Is that what's really going on here?

PAUL. Yes.

> (**DONNA** *is shocked.*)
>
> (*Finally:*)

DONNA. Do you want out of this family?

PAUL. No.

DONNA. Then stop acting like it.

PAUL. Stop acting…what? Disappointed? Is that it? We can have a happy marriage as long as I pretend everything's okay and go through the motions? Just keep pretending it's okay to "reimagine" our backyard and our house every few years? Just keep pretending we know just who the hell that person we call our son is when we don't? You said yourself we don't even know what he would want for a birthday present. You were really onto something when you said that, Donna. We may not know him at all. You want to deny all that? I don't remember that in our vows. "In sickness and in health, in absolute denial"…no, sorry don't remember that part.

DONNA. Selfish. You're so selfish, Paul.

PAUL. Let's just speak it aloud. Our son is lost.

DONNA. Don't say that. Don't you say that to me, Paul.

PAUL. It's true.

(**DONNA** *gets up from her chair.*)

DONNA. I'm not sitting down with you.

(**DONNA** *begins pacing.*)

PAUL. Everything I do, every time I say something to Jess it comes back at me with so much venom and spite attached to it, I barely recognize him and the only thing that labels him – that defines him as my son – is the gut pain I feel every time he acts out.

DONNA. I'm not listening to you, Paul.

(**PAUL** *stands up from his chair.*)

PAUL. Pain is the only commonality.

DONNA. Stop feeling sorry for yourself, would you?

PAUL. The boy we never knew is gone, Donna, and even after we commit him and clean him up, he still won't be coming home and I'm so tired of hurting all the time because of it. Feeling guilty because of it.

DONNA. Oh, so we never knew our son and now we're the reason he's messed himself up?

PAUL. We're responsible.

DONNA. We're his parents, we're always going to wonder if we did enough and even if we did do enough we'll still find a way to blame ourselves for it. You said as much yourself.

PAUL. This is different. This isn't about "what we did or didn't do." This is who we are.

DONNA. You're not making any sense.

PAUL. Think about it. My father was an alcoholic. Your brother is manic-depressive. Our genes mixed up this insane cocktail that makes our son compelled to do drugs. That's on us.

DONNA. (Overlapping.) Oh, for God's sake, Paul. That's... that doesn't mean...anything...that is just nonsense!

PAUL. (Overlapping.) And, what's worse, we set all this in motion and now we can't even stop him because of our own limitations. We can't even talk to our own child like he's our child because we don't even know him. He might as well be someone else's kid.

DONNA. I am not limited!

PAUL. Just because we made him, doesn't mean we know him. It's arrogant to think that. That's such an arrogant thought.

DONNA. Speak for yourself.

PAUL. I see this all so clearly now. Our gene pool mapped out this little trap for him to walk into and we're so broken now because of it...we're so tainted in our own thinking processes...our own presumptions about who he is and what he needs...just overflowing with NA and AA and Al-Anon and every other "go-fuck-yourself-on-paper" bullshit dogma that we have forgotten how to talk to our kid like he was our child and not a problem we have to fix. Not a bathroom to paint. A yard to "reimagine."

DONNA. Oh, is that what this is about, too? I knew it...

PAUL. *(Overlapping.)* We're so broken and damaged that we think our drug-addicted son is an appliance. We think he comes with blueprints.

DONNA. *(Overlapping.)* ...You are resentful of all the work I wanted to do on the house...excuse me for trying to do something nice for us.

PAUL. *(Overlapping.)* We're going to pay some rehab facility to take him away from us and just handle it. Our son is dry cleaning. Our son is the car in the shop.

DONNA. He's not a fucking car!

PAUL. *(Not listening.)* And even if we do get him off drugs, he's still gone.

DONNA. Stop saying that!

PAUL. I can't relate to him, Donna. Maybe I've never been able to relate to him.

DONNA. He's not gone!

PAUL. He's like an alien to me. Maybe that's always been true and I'm just now noticing.

DONNA. He's our son!

PAUL. He doesn't even look like our son anymore! He doesn't look like Jess! He's twenty pounds skinnier, his face is all scabbed up. His teeth...all that money on braces and he does that to his teeth? He's got all that... *rot* all over his mouth now.

DONNA. We can fix that.

PAUL. He doesn't even sound like himself anymore, Donna – all that yelling. He's permanently hoarse. He doesn't act like Jess – our son never would have taken a swing at you.

DONNA. We can have our son back!

PAUL. We don't know who our son even is. We can get him off drugs but somewhere between us planning his entire education and endlessly renovating this house he became someone we never met.

DONNA. You're giving up.

PAUL. Not true. I'm still committed to helping him.

DONNA. What you're saying is failure. It's surrender.

PAUL. I think we should adjust our expectations.

DONNA. I'm not giving up on our son just because you feel guilty!

PAUL. Why can't you ever hear what I'm saying?

DONNA. You're abandoning him.

PAUL. I am doing no such thing.

DONNA. In your heart, you're giving up.

PAUL. If you would actually listen –

DONNA. No, I'm not listening to this garbage anymore. Shut up, shut up, shut up!

PAUL. No, I won't shut up! You couldn't get me to shut up now if your life depended on it!

(DONNA *picks up her chair and throws it at* PAUL, *barley missing him.*)

What the hell's the matter with you? Don't you throw that chair at me. Who the hell are you to throw that chair at me? I bought that chair. Don't you dare throw that chair at me.

DONNA. Fine, I'll throw *this* one at you.

(DONNA *goes for* PAUL's *chair and picks it up.*)

PAUL. Don't Donna. Don't you do that.

DONNA. Stop talking like that about our son.

PAUL. I'm telling you what I feel is true.

DONNA. It is not true, you sonofabitch!

PAUL. I feel it is.

DONNA. No, it's not true. He comes home. We get him help. He's our son again. That's the truth, Paul. That's the truth and you're going to say it.

PAUL. I can't say it if I don't believe it.

DONNA. Yes, you can!

PAUL. I won't.

DONNA. *(Brandishing the chair menacingly.)* Say it!

PAUL. Don't you throw that, Donna.

DONNA. Say it, Paul! Say our son's going to be okay!

PAUL. No!

>(**DONNA** *throws the chair at* **PAUL,** *this one getting even closer to him.)*

Goddamn it, Donna! You could have hurt me!

DONNA. I don't care!

PAUL. You could've broken the chair.

>(**DONNA** *grabs a nearby potted plant, a fern.)*

Whoa, hold on, hold on. Not the fern, Donna. My mother gave us that.

DONNA. Fuck your mother! According to you, her genes got us into this whole mess.

>(**DONNA** *hurls the fern at* **PAUL.** *This time it comes dangerously close to him, ultimately breaking.)*

PAUL. Oh yeah? You want to play that? You want to break stuff?

DONNA. I'm not afraid of you.

PAUL. I will break that fucking fairy.

DONNA. You couldn't pick it up if you tried.

PAUL. I will throat kick that stupid, new-age fuck-monkey until its head comes right off, Donna!

>(**PAUL** *charges upstage toward the fairy.* **DONNA** *races toward him.)*

DONNA. Don't you do that, Paul!

PAUL. I'll kick it to fucking pieces, Donna!

DONNA. You leave her alone!

>(**DONNA** *grabs* **PAUL,** *who in turn grabs her.)*

PAUL. Our son is going to die!

(The two of them stand there, looking at each other, breathing heavily, until:)

(Once again, a light from a neighboring yard turns on.)

DONNA. See what you did?

PAUL. I don't care. I'm tired of hiding.

(PAUL pulls away from DONNA and walks over to the end of the yard, toward the light.)

(He grabs a chair and brings it over to the fence, standing on it in order to see better.)

DONNA. Paul, what are you doing?

PAUL. Tired of being embarrassed.

DONNA. Paul, whatever you think you're thinking of doing...*don't.*

PAUL. Hello, Mrs. Johnston.

DONNA. Great.

(Vague mumbling is heard from Mrs. Johnston.)

PAUL. Yes, that's right. It's my wife and I making all the noise. We made all the noise before but we hid when you came out the first time.

DONNA. We're very sorry, Mrs. Johnston.

(Vague mumbling from Mrs. Johnston.)

PAUL. Well, I don't know, really. Define "late."

DONNA. Paul.

(Vague mumbling from Mrs. Johnston.)

PAUL. No, I think there's an argument about that. Somewhere in the world it is a "reasonable hour."

DONNA. Would you stop taunting her?

(Vague mumbling from Mrs. Johnston.)

PAUL. Well, we're fighting because our son isn't home. Again.

DONNA. *(Overlapping.)* Everything's fine, Mrs. Johnston. Paul, stop it.

PAUL. *(Overlapping.)* You see, Mrs. Johnston, he's on drugs and we're waiting for him to come home so we can take him to rehab.

DONNA. *(Overlapping.)* Dammit, Paul!

PAUL. *(Overlapping.)* And, since we don't have sex anymore…

DONNA. *(Overlapping.)* Don't do this!

PAUL. *(Overlapping.)* …And we've just about remodeled and reorganized our home into oblivion, we're now fighting with each other just to pass the time. Does that make you happy, you nosey little dwarf?

DONNA. She doesn't deserve your abuse, Paul. Mrs. Johnston, we're very sorry…

(More vague mumbling from Mrs. Johnston.)

PAUL. Oh really? Priceless. That's interesting to hear you say that.

DONNA. What?

(More vague mumbling from Mrs. Johnston.)

PAUL. Wow, is that so? Fascinating stuff, Mrs. Johnston.

DONNA. What's she saying?

PAUL. She's saying, that not only is she going to consider removing us from the planning committee but she's not surprised Jess is doing drugs seeing how we behave.

(DONNA impulsively charges the fence.)

DONNA. Go fuck yourself you old, wrinkled cunt!

PAUL. Troll!

DONNA. Who the fuck do you think you are?

(More vague mumbling is heard from Mrs. Johnston. This round is louder, though, more intense.)

What's she saying now?

PAUL. We're definitely off the planning committee and she's going to call the police.

DONNA. Good! That committee sucks ass!

PAUL. You hear that? We don't want to be on your stupid, ass-sucking planning committee anyway. And, hey – go right ahead, call the police. I'm begging you to call the police because then I can tell them how you still receive social security checks from dead Mr. Johnston. Yeah, didn't think I knew about that, huh? That's right.

DONNA. She really does that?

(**PAUL** *nods.*)

PAUL. Oh and Mrs. Johnston? Just so we're clear. I think Saint Rocco is the most unnecessary saint ever invented in the history of the Catholic Church!! That's right! How do you like that? How does that work for you? He's totally extraneous and I suspect...a little bit *guido.* That's right, Mrs. Johnston...he's got a little New Jersey in him! Which reminds me, speaking of the Garden State, the Church has so many saints, it's a shame there's no saint for yard maintenance because we'd be praying to that saint right now – on our hands and knees at the forest of plant and scum that is your backyard, Mrs. Johnston. Oh, wait a minute, I forgot. We can't do that. We can't get on our hands and knees to pray to that hypothetical Catholic saint. Do you know why, Mrs. Johnston? Because we're not Catholic! That's right, we lied during our interview just to get on the planning committee! Nope. There's not a confessional booth between us! We're Episcopalian! Yeah, that's right, Mrs. Johnston. Episcopalian – the other white Christians! We're the ones without all the lawsuits. So why don't you go back in your house and pray to all your needless saints, and continue to defraud the American government while we get on, waiting for our son, in the land of the living and legal!

(**DONNA** *charges the fence.* **PAUL** *steps down from the chair and grabs at his stomach, grimacing and moving away from the fence.*)

DONNA. And another thing! Your name is Claire! Fucking Claire! No more Mrs. Johnston. I don't care what generation you only partially evolved out of! From now on your name is cock-sucking, butt-fucking, shit-stinking Claire!

(A door is heard slamming and a light goes out.)

DONNA. That showed her.

(PAUL starts to pace around the yard, holding his stomach. DONNA turns around and sees PAUL.)

What's wrong? Paul? What's the matter?

PAUL. My stomach.

DONNA. Are you okay?

PAUL. My IBS is acting up.

DONNA. Do you need to go to the bathroom?

PAUL. No. It just hurts.

DONNA. Breathe. Just try and breathe.

PAUL. It's like I swallowed a basketball.

DONNA. Just try and calm down a little.

PAUL. It's killing me.

DONNA. Here sit down.

PAUL. Feel like it's going to explode.

DONNA. Just breathe.

PAUL. I'm breathing.

DONNA. Then breathe some more.

(DONNA rights one of the chairs and sits PAUL down.)

You breathing?

PAUL. Stop telling me to breathe.

DONNA. Are you breathing?

PAUL. Yes.

DONNA. Okay. Just breathe.

PAUL. Okay.

(For a moment the two of them sit down, breathing, until:)

"Old, wrinkled, cunt"?

DONNA. You don't talk about someone's family like that.

PAUL. No.

DONNA. How did she look when you told her we were Episcopalian?

PAUL. Like I slapped the Virgin Mary.

DONNA. Good.

PAUL. Very.

DONNA. How did you know about her husband's Social Security checks?

PAUL. The mailman put it in our box by mistake once.

DONNA. That guy.

PAUL. I know, he still makes the same mistake after all this time. You'd think it was simple enough. We're 34. She's 34B. Basic stuff, right?

DONNA. We are talking about the Post Office.

PAUL. I wasn't even thinking about it when I opened it... pieced it back together as best I could and put it in her mailbox.

DONNA. You should turn her in.

PAUL. Yeah, well...

(*A quiet settles back down, until:*)

DONNA. How's your stomach?

PAUL. On fire.

DONNA. Keep breathing.

(*Another quiet settles in, until:*)

PAUL. She had a bird bath in there.

DONNA. What's that?

PAUL. Amongst all the other debris she had an antique looking bird bath.

DONNA. Huh. How does it look?

PAUL. It looks nice. Very fashionable.

(**DONNA** *walks over to the fence, steps up on the chair, and peeks over.*)

DONNA. Oh, yeah. Hey, that's really cute.

PAUL. It is.

> (DONNA *steps off the chair. She grabs the chair and*
> *moves it back to its original spot. She sits down.*)

DONNA. Maybe we should get one of those. That might be a good idea for back here. We could put it right over by the waterfall. What do you think?

PAUL. I think it would be a terrible idea. All that standing water. The mosquitos. It would turn into a West Nile virus breeding ground.

DONNA. Oh, you're right. We should tell her about that. That affects us, too.

PAUL. Let her calm down a little first. We'll give her a couple of days. Then we can mention it.

DONNA. You're probably right.

> (*Quiet settles, until:*)

That does give me an idea, though.

PAUL. Uh-oh.

DONNA. No, no, this is good. We should get one of those things that collect rainwater. You know, for the plants? You put it right under the gutter.

PAUL. A rain barrel?

DONNA. Exactly. We can get a rain barrel. They make them very cute and rustic looking, too. It would look nice out here.

PAUL. Mosquitos wouldn't get in there?

DONNA. No, you can put a wire mesh cover over the top that would keep them out.

PAUL. Huh. That does sound nice.

DONNA. And it would be very green.

PAUL. Rain barrel.

DONNA. Rain barrel. Yeah.

> (*Quiet settles again.*)
> (*Finally:*)

PAUL. I don't think he's coming tonight.

DONNA. No.

> *(Again, quiet, until:)*

You really think we don't know our own son?

PAUL. I know I don't know him. Do you?

DONNA. I don't understand what he's doing. I've never fully got where he was coming from but...to say I don't know him at all seems...

PAUL. He's not like us.

DONNA. Does that matter? Does he have to be like us for him to be our son? For us to help him?

PAUL. No, it doesn't mean that. And, for the record, I'm not giving up. I'm not surrendering. I am still committed to getting him help.

DONNA. You just don't think it will do any good.

PAUL. I'm starting to have my doubts.

> *(Some more quiet settles.)*

DONNA. You really think we've lost him?

PAUL. I do. I don't know if that makes it true. It's how I feel. I wish I didn't feel this way... I hate it that I... I'm not particularly proud that this is how I feel about it but...

> *(They continue to sit there, waiting.)*

> *(Finally:)*

DONNA. I was in the living room the other day doing a little "advanced cleaning" with the dustbuster...really getting into the corners...and I had to move part of the couch to get at this absolutely prehistoric dust bunny and I found that little patch of discolored carpet... remember that?

PAUL. From the wine?

DONNA. *(Nodding.)* Jess was so little then...he came charging into the room all excited, wearing mismatched pajamas – orange and blue, it was just horrible – and he came in horsing around with that plastic toy guitar we had bought him...and he accidentally knocked over your wine.

PAUL. He felt so bad about that.

DONNA. That's what I was thinking about. How awful he felt. How it became like a mission for him to get that red wine stain out of the carpet. We tried all those cleaning products...we even let him try to bleach it... of course it just faded it and then we decided just to move the couch over it to cover it, so we didn't have to see it...so he didn't feel so bad about it every time he walked into the living room.

PAUL. Your friend, Kira, the "feng shui" expert...

DONNA. *(Overlapping.)* Oh my God, that's right...

PAUL. *(Overlapping.)* ...She got all bunched about it...said we were ruining the "flow" of our house by moving the couch over a few inches like that. She was so mad at us about that.

DONNA. She was.

PAUL. What was it she said we were doing?

DONNA. She said not promoting a healthy flow in our living area was the equivalent of not "fluffing our chakras."

PAUL. God bless non-fluffed chakras.

(They laugh a small laugh for a moment.)

DONNA. Once I finished cleaning, I started putting everything away and it wasn't until I started making dinner that I realized that the incident with the carpet was the first "pleasant Jess" anecdote I'd recalled by myself in a long time that wasn't followed up with a sucker punch. The first time I thought about him when I was alone, unguarded and didn't have my stomach turn into knots by some other less than pleasant memory of how he is now.

PAUL. Yeah.

DONNA. Our son was born here. This house is filled with great "remember when" stories...and yet it's like I've blocked so many of them out.

PAUL. I have, too.

DONNA. *(Pointing.)* That part of the yard right over there where we caught him trying to "dig to China." The butterfly sticker we put on the glass sliding door because Jess kept walking into it and we tried not to laugh but it was so funny when he did it…

PAUL. Even he thought it was funny after awhile.

DONNA. The constellation of stars he put on the ceiling in his bedroom…the hours he must have spent in his room…looking up at them.

(DONNA *looks over at* PAUL. *Then, confessing:*)

I've suppressed the urge to enjoy so many good memories because I know, sooner or later, it just brings me right back to more recent ones and I can't live through that transition anymore. I can't start thinking about one wonderful memory about our boy only to have it invaded by another memory kicking me in the gut. It takes so much out of me and I can't…breathe through that anymore.

PAUL. Yeah.

DONNA. But now, all the good things about him…all the things that make him…that make me…feel…it's like I've dismantled a bridge to those places for my own good…and I can't get back to them…and it just…

(DONNA *looks around the yard.*)

(Finally:)

I don't want to do this anymore.

PAUL. Should we call it a night?

DONNA. No, I mean, I don't want to do any of this anymore. I don't want to wait for him anymore. I don't want every waking moment to be about him…worrying for him. I don't want to do that anymore.

PAUL. We don't have to make any definitive decisions about this right –

DONNA. You said earlier we may share blame in this because of who we are…our genes…our limitations…

PAUL. Well, that's... I was only saying that's... I feel that way.

DONNA. Maybe you're right. Maybe we gave him bad genes that helped him walk down this path. Maybe we inadvertently led him to this place and then abandoned him with our own incompetence and we can't help him now because we don't know him well enough to reach him. Maybe you're right, maybe all that's true. But none of it matters.

PAUL. It doesn't?

DONNA. Our son is going to die in a ditch or he's going to clean himself up and either of those scenarios will play themselves out no matter what we do. No matter how many rehabs we send him to, no matter how many fist fights you get into with him, no matter how many times we clean and renovate this house, no matter how many times he...

    (Almost breaking up.)

...tries to choke me. No matter how long we stay out here waiting for him. No matter how many memories we suppress. The truth is...nothing we do will change what he has in store for himself.

PAUL. Then why are we still out here?

    (Silence. No answer, or maybe the quiet is its own answer. More quiet ensues, until finally:)

Sometimes... I fuck my computer.

DONNA. I know. I caught you once.

PAUL. Oh. Shit.

DONNA. It's okay.

PAUL. You didn't say anything?

DONNA. I didn't want to embarrass you. Besides, it was cute.

PAUL. Cute?

DONNA. It was like a *National Geographic* special. "The North American Middle-Aged Male At Rest." It was quite informative.

PAUL. Happy to help.

DONNA. Nice technique.

PAUL. Okay, enough.

DONNA. Is it better by yourself?

PAUL. Of course not.

DONNA. What's the attraction?

PAUL. It's less complicated. Watching other people do it.

DONNA. Is that what's complicated about us?

PAUL. I don't know...

DONNA. Don't you miss us?

PAUL. I do and when we're together...

> (*Quiet.*)

You are still that girl, you know?

DONNA. Am I?

PAUL. You're still the one I met all those years ago. The one I told all those stupid pick-up lines to. The one who had mercy on me and decided to drink all those diet sodas with me.

DONNA. Only to discover you were allergic to Aspartame.

PAUL. Four antihistamines later.

> (*This sits there.*)

It was you and I back then.

DONNA. I know.

PAUL. We can have that again.

DONNA. We have it now, Paul.

PAUL. Really? This is it?

> (**DONNA** *stops for a moment, considering something.*)
>
> (*Finally:*)

DONNA. We wanted each other. We wanted a boy. We wanted a house.

> (**DONNA** *looks around the backyard for a moment.*)

DONNA. We asked, we received.

(This sits there.)

DONNA. This is it, Paul. The rest is up to us.

PAUL. What if that's not good enough?

DONNA. What do you want? Everything wrapped with a bow? Maybe *you* need to adjust *your* expectations and if you can't see that...if you want to give up?

PAUL. I'm not giving up? Did I say I was giving up?

DONNA. You know where the front door is.

PAUL. Which one? We've gone through five of them.

DONNA. I'm serious.

> (**PAUL** *takes all of this in.*)
>
> (*More quiet ensues. This time, it doesn't seem so painful.*)
>
> (*Finally:*)

PAUL. What do we do? I mean now. What do we do right now?

DONNA. If we're still awake when the stores open, we'll buy some Genteel Pearl, pick out some nail-up tin ceiling tiles. We can even look for some pool accessories. If he doesn't come home by then, maybe we'll paint the bathroom. Maybe we'll just go to sleep.

PAUL. In the meantime?

DONNA. We wait.

> (**PAUL** *nods. The two continue to sit, waiting for their son. After a moment, they hold hands.*)
>
> (*Lights out.*)

End of Play